The Werewolf at Home Plate

by Bill Doyle
Illustrated by Jared Lee

Scholastic Inc.
New York   Toronto   London   Auckland
Sydney   Mexico City   New Delhi   Hong Kong

For Nan Vincent—the mom at home plate.
—B.D.

To Cousin Billy Fiock.
—J.L.

ISBN 978-0-545-34198-1

12 11 10 9 8 7 6 5 4 3 2 1   11 12 13 14 15 16/0

Printed in the U.S.A.   40
First printing, September 2011

Book design by Jennifer Rinaldi Windau

CHAPTER 1

"Dude, You Look Like a Poodle"

Karl's paws had never moved so fast.

As he raced to the outfield, ten other werewolves snapped at his tail.

"No way you'll get that ball!" one growled.

Just watch me, Karl thought, sprinting faster. *I'm like the wind.*

"Not going to happen!" shouted another werewolf. It was Alphonse, a tough cub from Karl's neighborhood.

Karl stuck out his baseball glove. Nothing anyone

could say would stop him from making this catch! Nothing!

Just then Alphonse said, "Dude, you look like a poodle."

That did the trick.

Whift! Karl's glove jerked the wrong way. As the ball whizzed past, he turned to grab it—

And lost his balance. He spun around like a lawn sprinkler. While he whirled, Karl had to admit his patchy coat *did* look like a poodle's. His mom said his fur would even out as he got older. For now, though, he looked ready for a fancy dog show—not the biggest night of his life.

Finally, Karl stopped spinning. He slammed snout-first into the turf. The other werewolves on the field howled. Normally, Karl would laugh, too. But Monster League tryouts were way too important to him. He wanted to be a Junior Club Werewolf more than anything.

On the sidelines, Coach Powers blew his whistle and marked his clipboard. "That's an F in fielding, Karl," he said.

Karl hopped up and trotted over. "Coach, it's not my fault that—"

Holding up a paw, Coach interrupted, "You know my motto, Karl."

"Don't make excuses on the diamond, just good plays." Karl's shoulders slumped.

Coach nodded. "You've got one more chance left," he said. "There's still hitting. Stay focused!"

In each of the six events at tryouts, Coach Powers gave them a grade. Cubs with at least a C average made the Junior Club Werewolves.

Cubs who didn't make the cut . . . well, Karl

didn't even want to think about *that*.

"Things aren't looking good for you, Poodle," Alphonse said. He pushed past Karl as they headed toward home plate.

"Not a problem," Karl fired back. He'd been practicing hitting for months with his dad.

As Karl waited on deck, he glanced around the stadium. He recognized kids from school trying out for the different teams. A couple zombies from his homeroom tossed a head around in left field. A bigfoot from science class had just slid into first base and was now eating it.

And over there—something danced in the corner of Karl's eye. What was it?

He turned his body. But whatever the thing was turned with him! It darted around, out of sight. Karl snarled and chased it. He ran around and around in a small circle. Finally, Karl gave up, exhausted. He couldn't catch the pesky thing.

He looked up, sweating and panting. Everyone stared at him.

"Uh, that thing you're chasing?" Alphonse said. "It's called your tail." He tossed the bat to Karl. "And it's your turn to hit."

Karl blushed. Chasing his own tail was one of the two things he did when he was freaked out.

As Karl stepped into the batter's box, he knew this was his last chance. *I'll get an A-plus on my swing,* he told himself. *And I'll make up for the other scores.*

Coach pitched the ball. Karl swung as hard as he could—

Yes! The bat connected with the ball with a *whack!* and the tiniest *squeak!*

The ball sailed out toward right field. Karl ran. He sprinted to first—and then past it. He kept running toward the outfield.

"Karl!" Coach shouted. "Stop!"

Karl didn't listen. He raced over to the ball, sank his teeth into it, and ran it back to the pitcher's mound. He dropped the ball at Coach's feet, wagging his tail. Coach picked up the ball and touched Karl. "You're out," he said.

"Karl's the only monster I know who can get himself out!" Alphonse called from home plate. The other werewolves howled again.

Karl snapped out of it. Fetching a squeaky ball was the *second* thing he did when he was nervous.

Ten minutes later, Coach Powers and the other coaches taped up the lists of the monsters that had made the different teams. Karl ran his paw down the Werewolf list, his heart pounding.

"Move over, Poodle, so the rest of us can see," Alphonse complained.

"Hold on," Karl said, starting to panic. He read the list of fifteen names again. And again. His name wasn't there!

He wasn't a JC Werewolf! Karl felt sick.

"Maybe next year, Karl," Coach Powers said,

patting him on the shoulder. "Now take a seat over there. I need to talk to the team about our first game."

"I'll just wait outside for my dad to pick me up," Karl tried to say. But he was so choked up that no words came out.

Karl padded toward the door with his tail tucked between his legs. He felt like all the monsters were watching him.

This can't be the end, he thought. *I have to find a way to be a JC Werewolf!*

CHAPTER 2
Alley of Losers

When Karl rushed outside, storm clouds were swirling overhead. But Karl didn't care if he got drenched and smelled like wet dog. Nothing could make him go back into the stadium.

Through the doors, he heard the Ghosts' coach shout, "Congratulations! You've made the team. You're going to have the most fun of your afterlives!"

Karl didn't want to hear any more. He ducked around the corner into the alley. Fumes from an open sewer grate filled the air, and the streetlight had blown out. It was the perfect dark and smelly spot to do some thinking.

How was Karl going to break the news to his dad? They'd planned to go for lice cream to celebrate Karl making the team. But now what?

Karl slumped miserably against a dumpster.

"Are you okay?" a voice asked. Except it sounded like "arshyousokash?"

Surprised, Karl jerked back. A plump vampire kid stepped out of the shadows. His huge fangs made him look a little like a walrus—and they dripped with drool.

"Um, sure, I'm okay," Karl said. "By the way, I just ate garlic. Or curry. Or shellfish. Or whatever you're allergic to."

The vampire laughed. Good thing Karl didn't care about getting wet. Spit sprayed out between the kid's fangs when he opened his mouth and laughed.

"No, I'm not hungry," the vampire said. "What am I saying? I'm *always* hungry. But the tryouts made me lose my appetite. I didn't make the

Vampire team and they—I'm babbling." He stuck out a chubby hand to shake Karl's paw. "Hey, I'm Dennis. Are you sure you're all right?"

"Not really." Karl sighed. "I'm Karl. I didn't make my team either."

"Huh," Dennis said. "I didn't know poodles had their own team."

Karl growled. "I am NOT a poodle!"

Poof! Dennis turned into a bat. And fell to the ground with a plop. His little wings flapped but couldn't lift his weight. He flopped around, squealing through his giant fangs. A second later, he popped back into a kid.

"Sorry," Karl said. He stepped toward Dennis, his foot coming down on a rock. "I didn't mean to scare you—"

"Ummph," the rock said.

Karl glanced down. The rock was a zombie girl's head!

"What's up?" she asked with a smile. Or was it a frown? Tricky to tell because her head was upside down.

Karl leapt off. "Why didn't you say something sooner?"

"Not easy with a werewolf's paw up your nose," the zombie said. "Patsy's my name, going to pieces my game. Can you give me a hand?"

Karl rolled her head right side up.

Patsy chuckled. "No, really—give me my hand. Both actually. My pal went to find my body parts, but he's been gone a while." She turned her mouth to the side and shouted, "Maxwell!"

A mummy kid stumbled around the corner into the alley. He was swimming in layers of cloth strips.

"Here I am," he said. "Don't lose your head, Patsy." He waved her hand in front of his face like a fan. Sweat stained his oversized wrappings.

"You're the best, Maxwell," Patsy said.

"I know," he said and sounded like he meant it. "Even if I didn't make the Mummies."

Maxwell put the hand down to her mouth. Patsy used her fingers to whistle. Hearing the call, her headless body popped up in the dumpster and climbed out. The body picked up her head and placed it on her neck with a little twist. Then she screwed her hand back in place.

"Well, it's been fun hanging out with other losers," Patsy said, "but I've got to get back to the grave."

"Hang on," Karl said. "I'm not a loser."

Patsy stopped. "Sorry," she said. "I didn't mean just you. None of us made our teams."

"I'm going to change that," Karl said. "I'm going to show everyone that I should be a JC Werewolf!"

"But they didn't want you on their team," Dennis said.

Karl looked at the other monsters and got an idea. "We can start our own team!"

"Ha," Maxwell said. "Very funny. We're the leftovers. And besides, there's never been a team made up of different kinds of monsters."

"It wouldn't have to be for long," Karl said, excited about the idea. "If we can win, everyone will see how good we are. They'll want us back. Then we can play with our real teams!"

Dennis counted out loud and said, "There's only four of us. We don't have enough players."

"I'd join." Mike, a swamp thing from Karl's school, crawled up out of the open sewer. He must have been hiding down there.

Before Karl could say anything, Beck, a bigfoot, climbed down from a nearby fire escape. "Me, too," Beck said.

"That's two more right there!" Karl said. "We can get more monsters who were cut from their teams to sign up." Karl stuck out his paw. "Come on, who's in?"

Patsy shrugged and put her decayed hand on top of his paw. Then, one by one, the others placed five pale fingers, a slimy tail, a sweaty bandaged hand, and a fist of sharp claws in the middle.

As they stood in a circle, Karl bounced his paw up and down and said, "Three cheers for the . . . hold on, our team needs a name."

Just then the storm finally broke. Lightning struck a lamppost out on the street. The blinding, bright flash made Dennis scream and turn into a bat.

"Good idea, Dennis," Karl said, grinning. "We'll be the Scream Team."

CHAPTER 3
Practice Is Not Perfect

Karl and the five other monsters met up the next night at the haunted bog. NO TRESPASSING! signs were everywhere. Slime-suckers oozed on the mushy ground, eating muck and releasing powerful gassy explosions. And, over it all, loomed the town's scariest mansion hanging on to the side of a cliff.

Patsy brought along two friends. She carried one of them in the basket on her bike. It was Eric the blob. She plopped him on the ground where he quivered like a jellyfish.

Her other friend was Bolt, a Frankenstein's monster who Karl knew from math class. His body parts came from different people, and sometimes they did their own thing. One of Bolt's arms had belonged to the teacher's pet. So he always raised his hand in class—even when he didn't know the answer.

"Okay, with Eric and Bolt, we've got eight monsters," Karl said. "We need nine, though, to fill all the positions."

Just then, a ghoulish screech filled the air.

"Blalllllaahshshhshshsh!" A shrieking ghost kid emerged from a tree stump and shot toward the monsters. Not one of them moved, not even Dennis.

"What's wrong with you?" the ghost demanded. "Aren't you scared? I will GOBBLE you up!"

"Don't think you've got room," Patsy said calmly. "Looks like you just ate lunch."

The ghost stopped. He glanced down at his see-through body to his stomach. A grilled cheese sandwich and parts of an apple sat there. He turned bright red. "Right," the ghost said, suddenly smiling.

"In that case, can I play with you guys? I'm J.D."

And just like that the Scream Team had nine players. All the monsters made a circle around Karl.

"Why are we practicing in a bog?" Mike the swamp thing asked. He scooped up a handful of mushy maggots and popped them in his mouth. "Squish bugs make good snacks, but not the best game surface."

"We can't use the real practice fields," Karl said. "The Scream Team isn't an official junior club of the Monster League."

Dennis was eating squish bugs now, too. "But they'll let us play baseball this season, right, Karl?" he asked, spraying spit and insect parts.

Karl didn't know. He'd gone online to the JC Monster League website. There didn't seem to be any rules against them forming their own team.

"We just need to win the first game in a few days," Karl said. "The real teams will see they've made big mistakes. And then they'll invite us back!"

Excited, all the monsters started talking at once.

Beck the bigfoot shouted above them, "Who's going to play what position, Karl?"

"Well, I'll be pitcher," Karl said. "And, the rest—"

"I'll handle it," Maxwell cut him off, trying to sound like a big shot. "You!" he shouted. "You will play center field." His wrappings were so twisted, Maxwell couldn't tell he was pointing at a tree stump.

Karl pinched himself to keep from laughing. "We'll worry about positions later," he said. "Let's just play some catch to get warmed up first."

The monsters broke up into smaller groups, and stood staring at each other. Something was missing....

"Uh," Mike finally said, "I think we need baseballs to play baseball."

Wolfsbane! Karl forgot to bring balls.

"We don't need baseballs," he said, his mind racing. "All the pros know you can practice with ..." He looked around quickly and his eyes landed on a pus-bag tree. "Pus bags!"

Karl rushed over and plucked a jiggly baseball-sized bag off the tree. The others grabbed a few, too.

"See? This is great!" He tossed his pus bag to Eric. It hit the blob and exploded all over him.

"Sorry!" Karl said. "That one was just a little ripe." He snagged another bag and this time tossed it to J.D. The ghost caught it and threw it back.

Before long, the pus bags were flying back and forth. *We're practicing!* Karl thought. *Well, kind of . . .*

Some of the players were having a tough time even with catch. Still unable to see, Maxwell threw blindly to Beck. The bigfoot shouted, "I got it!" and ran like he was wearing flippers. By the time he got there on his huge flopping feet, the pus bag had landed and crawled away.

Mike was partners with Eric the blob. The pus

bags were so slimy from Mike's tail that they slid right off Eric.

Meanwhile, J.D. was throwing straight to Karl's mitt, but Karl couldn't get it to stay there!

"Must be a faulty pus bag," Karl said. But J.D. didn't have a problem with it. He caught every throw. Karl wanted to be pitcher more than ever. He was way better at throwing than catching.

After Karl dropped his sixth pus bag, he looked around the bog. Practice had gone downhill fast. Bolt was playing with a baby vulture. Maxwell was bossing around a shrub he thought was a monster. And Dennis gnawed on a rotting, wet log as a snack.

"Karl, this isn't working," Patsy said, heading to her bike. "Plus, I have a test tomorrow on famous beheadings." The other monsters started to follow Patsy back to the road.

"Wait!" Karl said, panicking. "Don't give up! We all want to play baseball and the Scream Team is our chance!"

"Then we've got a real conundrum on our

hands," Patsy called back. "Because without a coach the Scream Team is nothing but a mess."

J.D. drifted over to them. "What'd you say? Coach Conundrum?" the ghost asked, turning bright white. "Where?"

"No, a conundrum," Maxwell told him. "It's like a puzzling question."

"Oh, whew," J.D. said. "I thought you were talking about the Conundrum brothers. That's their mansion right there."

"The Conundrums live there?" Karl said, gazing in wonder up at the scary house.

"Sure," J.D. said. "Or they did. My family's been haunting this bog for years, and I've never actually seen them. They put up the No Trespassing signs and they're supposed to be terrifying."

Karl grinned. "J.D., you might have just found the answer to our problem," he said. "And it's another Conundrum."

CHAPTER 4
Ding-Dong Pitching

Karl led Patsy, Dennis, and J.D. across the bog. The rest of the team had stayed behind to practice. Maxwell said he'd whip the team into shape.

As they hiked toward the spooky mansion, Patsy picked up small skull grubs and batted their hard shells with a stick. The grubs cackled with a "phee-he!" as they flew into the distance. Karl thought she had a pretty good swing.

"So who are these scary Conundrum brothers anyway?" Patsy asked.

"Back in the day," Karl said, "they coached all the greats. Like Necroface, Gnomeneck, and, of course, Wolfenstein!"

"Wolfen-who?" Dennis asked.

Karl couldn't believe his ears. "Are you kidding? You don't know Wolfenstein? The most amazing Werewolf athlete of all time?"

Dennis nodded. But Karl saw he didn't know.

"I'll tell you about Wolfenstein," Karl said. "The Werewolves and the Ghosts were slugging it out in the Globe Series. All tied up at the bottom of the ninth with two outs, the Ghosts had the bases loaded. As Wolfenstein went to bat, he pointed a paw to the center-field bleachers. The stadium went crazy. No one had ever been gutsy enough to call

a shot like that. But guess what? Wolfenstein hit a home run."

J.D. added, "He said the Coaches Conundrum gave him the confidence to play like that."

Impressed, Patsy whistled. "And you think these big-shot brothers will want to coach us?"

Karl shrugged. "I hope at least one of them will. *If* they're still alive." When J.D. nudged him, Karl quickly added, "Not that there's anything wrong with being un-un-dead, Patsy. I mean, you know—" He was stammering again.

"No problem, Karl," Patsy said and laughed.

They reached the Conundrums' mansion. The house sprawled against the cliff with a wide moat of slime around it. Mini mouth-monsters slithered on the surface, using their tongues to paddle through the muck. The drawbridge that led to the front door was up. They had no way across.

"Coach Conundrum!" Karl yelled. But the mansion was made of heavy stone with no windows. No one inside would hear him.

"There's a doorbell next to the door," J.D. said. "I bet we can throw a rock at it and make it ring."

"Great idea," Karl said. They hunted around for stones and started throwing them at the doorbell. They all missed, bouncing into the moat with goopy splashes. The mouth-monsters slithered over and crushed the rocks with their teeth.

Ka-klink! Ka-klink! The sound came from behind them. Karl turned around. "Oh no," he said.

Trash-gobblers were crawling out of their holes in the bog and waddling toward them. The creatures' teeth glinted in the moonlight.

"They must have heard the rocks banging on the wall," J.D. said. "They're hoping it's dinner!"

Karl and his teammates were fenced in, backed up against the moat—and the mouth-monsters below.

"We need to hit that doorbell!" Karl said, and started throwing rock after rock. All their pitches missed the mark.

Dennis threw one of the last rocks. As it left his hand, there was a squeak. Without thinking, Karl's ears pointed up, and he started chasing it.

"No!" Patsy reached to stop Karl, and her arm tore off. Karl kept rushing to the moat. The hand crawled down to his leg and yanked his foot out from under him.

Finally, Karl snapped out of it.

"Uh, thanks, Patsy," Karl said.

"No problem." She screwed her arm back on. "Well, maybe a problem."

The trash-gobblers were even closer. *Phfft!* Dennis turned into a bat. Karl was starting to think they should just jump in and take their chances with the mouth-monsters.

There was one rock left. J.D. picked it up and

turned white with fear. Karl could see his heart pounding inside his body. Based on the heartbeat, he could tell how J.D. was going to throw it.

"A little harder," Karl said.

J.D. nodded and threw the rock. It was an amazing pitch with a corkscrew in the middle. The rock whizzed across the moat. Like a dart zeroing in on the bull's-eye, it smacked into the doorbell.

Ding-dong!

Even through the stone walls, they could hear someone shout angrily inside. With a rattling of chains, the bridge came slamming down toward them so fast the monsters had to jump back.

They hurried across the bridge to the front door. The trash-gobblers retreated, as if they didn't want to get any closer to the mansion—or the monsters that might be inside.

"Nice throw, J.D.," Karl said, catching his breath. "Are you guys okay?"

The others nodded. They all turned toward the door and waited.

With heavy grinding, the bolts of the door slid back. The rusty hinges screamed as the huge front door opened slowly.

Karl started to ask, "Is Coach Conundrum at home—?"

His snout snapped shut. Dennis shrieked.

What answered the door was the last thing any of them had expected.

CHAPTER 5
Coaches Conundrum

Maybe those mouth-monsters in the moat aren't so bad, Karl thought.

The figure in the doorway had two heads. And it was three times as tall as Karl.

"Check it out, Karl," Patsy whispered. He followed her gaze to the monster's giant feet. It was wearing footie pajamas with patterns of baseballs.

"You threw rocks at our house!" One of the heads yelled. Its face was angry and topped by a crew cut.

The other head grinned. "Hey there, gang!"

Its ponytail bobbed around as it nodded at them. "What's up?"

The angry head snapped around to glare at the grinning one. "What are *you* doing here?"

Rolling his eyes, the smiling head said, "Chill, bro." Then he turned to the Scream Team. "I'm Virgil Conundrum. And this cranky-pants is my brother, Wyatt."

Karl had only seen pictures of the Conundrums' heads—not their body. He hadn't known they were a two-headed monster. And from the looks on his teammates' faces, neither had they.

"Sorry my brother's being totally uncool," Virgil said. "We haven't seen guests—or each other—in five years. He's a little rusty in the welcome department."

"You haven't seen your brother for five *years*?" Patsy asked. She took off an ear and looked at it to make sure it wasn't clogged with wax.

Wyatt huffed impatiently. "The mansion is split down the middle. Virgil stays on his side. I stay on mine!"

Karl wondered how that would work.

"And all visitors stay away!" Wyatt added and tried to close the door.

Virgil held it open. As the brothers pushed back and forth on the door, Virgil asked Karl, "So what can we do you for? You kids selling organ cookies? You got any spleen mint? That's my fave!"

Karl shook his head. "My friends and I are starting a JC Monster League team. We're the Scream Team and we need a coach—or coaches."

"That's an awesome idea!" Virgil said.

"You're different kinds of monsters," Wyatt said. "You can't start a Junior Club team. Besides, our coaching days are over. Too many spies!"

"Spies?" J.D asked.

"Years ago, we coached different teams," Wyatt answered. "But somehow my brother knew all my secret plays and starting lineups!"

Virgil said, "And what's hilarious is somehow Wyatt knew mine, too!"

"Uh, you share the same body, right?" J.D. asked.

"Yes," Wyatt said.

"And your point is . . . ?" Virgil asked. "Anyway, I'd love to check out your team. If I like what I see, I'll coach you. This could be spectacular!"

Wyatt struggled harder to close the door. "I'm not going anywhere. I'm going back upstairs to reorganize my blister collection."

With a wink, Virgil leaned his head closer to Karl and his friends.

"You are?!" he said in a loud, fake whisper. "Your friends are having a party and we're invited?"

Karl had no idea what he was talking about. But he winked back and nodded.

Wyatt stopped trying to close the door. "Well," he said, "maybe I can go. . . . I guess I can organize my blisters later."

"Yes!" Karl said. "Thank you!"

"Don't thank me yet," Virgil said, patting his shoulder. "I'll make a final decision after I check out your team."

The Conundrums put on a sweat suit and followed the kid monsters back across the bog.

When they arrived, it was clear the rest of the Scream Team was sick of Maxwell. He was stuck in the branches of a dead tree, looking like an exploded roll of toilet paper. Karl and J.D. helped him down.

"Is that your idea of party decorations?" Wyatt snipped. "A mummy in a tree?"

"Chill, bro," Virgil said. He pulled out a baseball from a pocket in his sweatpants. "Let's see what these monsters have to offer."

Karl clapped his paws together. "We'll show you what we've got."

"We will?" Patsy asked. "I'd like to see that, too."

Karl asked the Conundrums to hit fly balls to the outfield. The monsters took turns catching them.

Virgil called, "Chatter, monsters! Talking is half the battle!"

"You should know about talking," Wyatt said. "That's all you do."

"*I* talk too much?" Virgil laughed. "You're the one who keeps telling people I'm adopted."

Karl took his turn in the outfield.

When the ball rocketed toward him, he stuck out his arm. The ball landed in his glove—

And bounced right out.

Wolfsbane! He'd forgotten to close the glove. His face stung with embarrassment.

Karl watched the others take their turns. One hit zinged toward Beck and Bolt.

"You got it, Bolt?" Beck asked.

"Got what?" Bolt asked, looking at Beck as if he was about to get a present. The ball sailed into his head.

Still, Karl held out hope the Conundrums would coach them. After all, Virgil was smiling ear to ear when he called them back to gather around.

"My goodness, that was—" Virgil burbled cheerily.

"—just awful," Wyatt finished for him. "Horrible, really. You call that party entertainment? The worst party ever. I mean, where's the cake?"

"But you'll coach us, won't you?" Karl asked, his heart sinking.

"Well, I would like—" Virgil started.

"Coach you?" Wyatt shouted. "So there's no party? I should have known this was a trick!"

He spun the Conundrums' body around so it was headed back to the mansion. Virgil dragged one leg, but Wyatt kept plowing ahead.

"I'm not coming out of retirement for this," Wyatt called over his shoulder. "And stay off our land!"

The brothers staggered away, bickering over who was taller. The monsters watched them go.

"Wow," J.D. said. "My parents were right. The Conundrums *are* scary."

"I need to get back to my coffin," Dennis said, tears mixing with the drool on his chin. "Is practice over?"

"You got it, bat boy," Maxwell said dismally. "And so is the Scream Team."

Karl clenched his fists. He shook his head. "No way."

"Come on, Karl, you heard the coaches," Patsy said. "They said we're horrible."

"It's not over," he said firmly. "Not until we're all playing on real teams again."

CHAPTER 6
Monster Rally

Three days later, the night of the Monster Rally arrived. All of the JC Monster League teams would be introduced.

Even if they didn't have a coach, Karl was determined the Scream Team would be at the rally tonight. J.D., Dennis, and Maxwell came over to Karl's house to prepare. He met them in the bushes in front and then snuck them around to his tree fort in the backyard.

Dennis was out of breath from the climb up the

ladder into the fort. He looked around with wide eyes. "Wow, it's a like a baseball museum in here."

A big poster of Wolfenstein hitting a home run was taped on one wall. In a small jar was the last tiny bite of a hot dog Karl had saved from a game last year. There was a piece of grass from the stadium's infield. Karl liked to open the jars just to get a whiff of the ballpark.

J.D. dropped the roll of fabric he'd lugged up the ladder. It hit the wood floor with a loud *crack!*

"Shhh!" Karl said. "My dad's in the house! He'll hear you!"

"So?" J.D. asked.

Karl said, "I haven't told him about not making the Werewolves."

"What?" Dennis asked, eyeing the hot dog in the jar. "Why not?"

"There's no reason to tell my dad, right?" Karl said, sliding the hot dog jar behind a box. "We still might be able to win the game in two days. Then Coach Powers and the other coaches will see how good we are and put us back on the real teams. Right?"

Karl knew this sounded pretty nuts. But it was his only chance to be on the Werewolves.

"I guess," J.D. said, sounding a little doubtful, too. To change the subject, he pointed at the fabric. "I found this burlap to make uniforms. It was in the trash at the cemetery."

Dennis felt the material. "That's coffin lining."

"I'll handle this," Maxwell announced. "I know how clothes should fit. I mean look at me." He gestured at the sweaty, drooping strips of cloth around his body.

The others thought he was kidding and laughed. But Maxwell was serious and the other monsters didn't have a clue how to sew. With no scissors in the fort, they used Dennis's fangs to cut the fabric and thread. It was a little soggy, but effective.

"To save time," Maxwell said, "let's just put our initials on the back of each uniform and a number."

"I'm going with number nine," Karl said,

stitching the circle of the nine on the fabric. "Just like Wolfenstein."

Dennis bit off the last thread just in time. They tossed the uniforms in a bag and rushed on their bikes to the stadium for the Monster Rally. Hundreds of kid monsters packed the stands, sitting together with their teams.

A stage had been set up in the middle of the baseball diamond. The teams' coaches and the president of the JC Monster League sat in a row of chairs behind the microphone.

The rest of the Scream Team was hiding behind a curtain in the back corner of the stage.

"Is everything set?" Karl asked, handing out the uniforms from the bag and putting on his own.

"Just completing Operation Name on List now." She waved her handless arm toward the stage. Her hand was crawling up the side of the podium. At the top, it grabbed a pen and scribbled the team's name at the top of the list.

Perfect timing. Dr. Neuron walked to the

podium. The place went crazy. He raised a tentacle for silence.

"Welcome, new teams of the JC Monster League!" Dr. Neuron said and his voice echoed throughout the stadium. "You carry on a proud tradition that includes Octopod, Wolfenstein, and Pussack. Tonight we usher you into the pack. As I read out your team name, please come to the stage."

He cleared his throat. "And now for our first team . . ." He squinted at the page. "What is this? Some kind of joke?" Dr. Neuron looked at the list again, and then said more like a question, "The Scream Team?" There was a sharp whine of the microphone. Monsters winced, and a few howled in pain.

With his teammates following, Karl burst from behind the curtain and trotted out on the stage. He was excited for Coach Powers to see him in his uniform.

As the Scream Team formed a line at the front of the stage, he waited for applause. But instead—*blam!* Laughter roared at them from the audience.

Dennis popped into a bat. J.D. turned bright red.

"Dream Team?" a Mummy shouted. "Like in your dreams team? Or bad dream team?"

"No, it's *Scream* Team," a Swamp Thing sneered. "Like scream for help because they're a bunch of losers."

A Ghost snickered, "Well at least that poodle kid got it right. He's a zero."

"It's the number nine," Karl called, and looked at his back. Uh-oh, it *was* a zero. He'd forgotten to sew the tail on the circle to make the nine.

Suddenly, Karl saw his team's uniforms for what they were. Burlap sacks with openings for heads and arms. They looked ridiculous.

It wasn't just Karl who was a target. The Bigfoots slid the rally programs on the ends of their toes and acted like they had Beck's flipperlike feet. The Blobs were quivering at Eric—and something about it was making him roll slowly back.

Coach Powers stormed over from the group of coaches. "Have you gone nuts, Karl?"

"We're a-a team—" Karl stammered. "We're the Scream Team."

Coach Powers cocked an eyebrow at him. "If you're a team, where's your coach?"

"We tried getting *two* coaches but one of them—" Karl started to say.

Coach Powers held up a paw. "You know how I feel about excuses, Karl. Now please leave the stage. And take these monsters with you."

Patsy turned to the president of the JCML. "Dr. Neuron, can't you help us?"

"I'm sorry," Dr. Neuron said. But he didn't sound like it. "The rules specifically say you need a coach."

With the crowd still hurling insults and laughter, the Scream Team started off the stage. Karl hesitated, and Dr. Neuron said firmly, "You heard me. No coach, no team."

"Then it's a good thing we're here," a voice said.

Karl's heart leapt. It was Virgil Conundrum! Shock swept through the crowd, as Wyatt and Virgil jogged up the steps and strode to the middle of the stage.

Wyatt glared at the audience until they quieted. Then he turned to Karl and his friends. "Where are you monsters going?" Wyatt demanded. "Come on back here and line up."

When they were in place at the front of the stage, Virgil announced, "We are the coaches of the Scream Team!"

The crowd gasped and there was a bit of scattered laughter. Dr. Neuron huddled with Coach Powers and the other coaches. One of them had the JCML rule book and flipped through it frantically.

Finally, Dr. Neuron walked back to the podium. "Fine," he said quietly. "The Scream Team . . ." No one clapped. "Okay, moving along! Next we have the Swamp Things!"

The stadium cheered, and the Scream Team hustled backstage.

"Way to go, team!" Virgil said and shared a few high fives.

"What changed your mind?" Karl asked Wyatt. "You think we're really good players after all, don't you?"

"Uh, no," Wyatt scoffed with a shake of his head. "It's because you're really, really bad and it's going to be hilarious to watch. I've coached the best in the game. Now I'll coach the worst!"

CHAPTER 7
Boo Camp

"If we're a real team now with real coaches," Bolt asked the night after the Monster Rally, "why are we still practicing *here*?"

Karl wondered the same thing. This was their first official practice. And the Coaches Conundrum had told them to meet back at the haunted bog.

"I'll tell you why," Coach Wyatt said. "Spies. We'll be safer from their prying eyes here."

"Besides, we live right there." Coach Virgil pointed to their mansion. "So our commute is wicked!"

"You kid monsters are too soft these days," Wyatt said. "We need to get the boo back in you! You've got to show the other teams you're tough!"

He tossed a base on the ground and stood next to it. "Imagine this is second base. You!" he shouted, pointing at Dennis. "Try to steal it!"

Dennis snatched up the base. He darted off and hid behind a stump. Virgil called him back and explained what it meant to steal a base in baseball.

"Let's try that again," Coach Wyatt said, putting the base back in place. "As you run toward the base, show me you're not afraid of me—or anything!"

Bolt went first and ran down an imaginary baseline. Coach Wyatt let out a scary yell. Bolt stopped on the spot. His leg that had belonged to a ballet dancer went up and did a little spin. Maxwell was next, and he gagged on his wrapping before reaching the base. And Patsy screamed her head off. Literally. Her head rolled down the baseline.

"All right," Wyatt said. "I've seen enough. Practice is over."

Karl and his teammates looked at each other. That was a baseball practice?

***

When they met up again the next night, the team trotted out into the heavy, dark mist that covered the haunted bog. There were shouts from Dennis and Maxwell. Someone had dug pits where first and second base should be—and the holes had spears sticking up at the bottom. The pitcher's mound had been replaced with quicksand.

If J.D. wasn't a ghost, he would've drowned.

"Who did this?" Mike asked.

Karl sniffed the ground and followed the scent to werewolf tracks. They led back to the road. "I'm

sure it was Alphonse," Karl said.

"It's not just the Werewolves, Karl," Patsy said. "The Zombies left this in my mailbox last night." She reached into her pocket. She pulled out a bottle of The Beast Glue Ever. "You know, ha-ha, because I always fall apart."

"And I got this," Dennis said, taking out a little toy baseball bat with legs and a head on it. "They call me Bat Boy."

"But aren't you?" Beck asked.

"Well, sure," Dennis said, sniffling a little. "But it's all how you say it."

The sounds of bickering came from across the bog. The Conundrums were arriving. "What's up, guys?" Virgil asked.

Before anyone could tell them about the notes or the sabotage, Wyatt barked, "Gather 'round, team! I have your positions figured out."

After the Conundrums tacked up a list on the pus-bag tree, the monsters rushed to read what positions they would play.

J.D. — Pitcher
Karl — Catcher
Patsy — Shortstop
Bolt — Center field
Dennis — 1st Base
Eric — 2nd Base
Maxwell — 3rd Base
Beck — Right field
Mike — Left field

Karl couldn't believe his eyes. *Catcher?* He hustled over to the Conundrums. "Coaches," he said, "I think there's a mistake. That list says I'm catcher."

Wyatt squinted at him. "No mistake. That's right."

"But," Karl lowered his voice, "I was hoping to be pitcher."

Wyatt frowned. "I keep hoping my brother will take a month-long trip far, far away. But that never happens either."

"It's just I'm not the world's best catcher," Karl said. "You've seen that."

"We haven't seen what you can do," Virgil said. "No one has." Karl waited for him to say more. But he just grinned.

Wyatt scoffed. "Just get out there and play. Work on pitching signals with J.D."

Hating every second of it, Karl swapped mitts with J.D. He put on the catcher's mask and chest protector. Karl crouched as if he were behind home plate and J.D. started throwing pitches.

They had been working on their signals for just a few minutes, when—

Ding! Ding! Ding! Karl's phone started ringing from the sideline. He trotted over to read the screen. His body went limp.

"What's wrong, Karl?" Patsy asked as the team gathered around.

Karl held up the cell phone. "It's an e-mail to all of us from the JC Monster League. It's the season schedule."

"Uh-oh," Dennis said. "Aren't we on it?"

"No, we're definitely on the schedule," Karl said, then he took a breath and added, "Our first game tomorrow night is against the Werewolves."

CHAPTER 8
Take Me Out of the Ball Game

The night of the season opener had arrived. The stadium was swept. The programs printed. The hot dogs steaming. The baselines drawn.

And Karl was hiding in his backyard fort, sprawled on the floor.

When his mom called him down for lunch, he told her he'd eaten bad roadkill. He said he felt sick, and if it was okay with her, he'd just stay up in his fort all day. Luckily, his dad was out of town on business so he didn't have to make up a story for him.

Karl's cell phone beeped. Another message from Patsy. She and J.D. had already texted him about thirty times.

Whr R u??? Game starts in 20 minutes!!!!

He typed back:

Not coming. Stomach hurts.

This was true. His stomach was a knot of nerves. But not because of roadkill.

Karl knew the Werewolves would destroy the Scream Team. He'd done everything this past week to get on the Werewolf team, not get run over by it. And what was worse, Coaches had made him catcher—the worst position for him. Everyone knew he couldn't catch. He might as well tie his hands behind his back and just wait for the world to laugh at him more.

When his cell phone beeped with another text, Karl turned it off and lay back down on the floor under his poster of Wolfenstein. Karl pulled his baseball cap lower so he couldn't see the poster.

He couldn't take it anymore. Karl decided to head to his room and go to bed. Tomorrow when he woke up, the game would be over and so would the Scream Team. His dream would be finished—but at least his life could go back to normal.

As he climbed down from his fort, his paw crunched down on something at the bottom of the ladder. It was a note. He unfolded it and read it.

Hey Karl,

I got home early from my business trip. Sorry you got a stomach full of bad roadkill. Figured I'd let you sleep. I'm going to the Werewolf game anyway. I'll talk to Coach Powers and let him know he'll have to put in a substitute for you.

Dad

Karl's stomach suddenly felt a lot worse. His dad was going to the game! He would find out the truth from Coach Powers—that Karl wasn't on the Werewolves. He had never actually said he was on the team. But he'd let his dad think that the practices were for the Werewolves.

That wasn't all. A word popped out from the note. *Substitute.* Karl felt even sicker.

Sure, the Werewolves had substitute players. But the Scream Team didn't. They were only nine. If Karl didn't show up, there wouldn't be enough players and his team would forfeit the game.

Karl had to get to the stadium! He'd try to find a way to fix everything—but he might already be too late. It was 11:50. The game would start in ten minutes. Any player that wasn't in line with his team at midnight wouldn't be allowed to play.

He ran to the front driveway, hopped on his bike, and started pedaling—but screeched to a halt. The eight other members of the Scream Team were biking down the street toward him.

"What are you guys doing here?" Karl said.

Patsy shrugged. "If you're not going to play, neither are we."

"This whole thing was your idea, Karl," Dennis said.

"I've changed my mind, guys," Karl said. "We have to play."

"Too late," J.D. said. "We can't get to the stadium on time on our bikes."

As Karl racked his brain for a solution, a van pulled over, and the Conundrums' heads popped out of the driver's side window.

"Did someone call for a cab?" Virgil said with a grin.

Wyatt snapped, "You always take the words out of my mouth!"

"Oh come on." Virgil rolled his eyes. "Go ahead and say it again, then."

"No, it's too late now," Wyatt said.

The Scream Team left their bikes on Karl's driveway and piled into the van. Karl sat next to Patsy in the far back seat.

"How'd they know to come to my house?" he asked her.

"I called them and told them to meet us here," Patsy said. "I had a feeling you'd change your mind."

Wham! They were tossed against the side of the van as it made a sharp turn one way and then the other.

The Conundrums both had shortcuts they wanted to take to the stadium, but they only had one set of hands.

"Take a left!" Virgil yelled.

"Take a right!" Wyatt yelled.

The van swerved back and forth, tossing the team around, but ended up going straight.

"Speed up!" and "Slow down!" the brothers shouted. And their feet pounded the gas and then brakes, and sometimes both at the same time.

Still, when the van bounced into the stadium parking lot, they had two minutes to spare. The clock over the entrance said 11:58. They sprinted inside.

Karl didn't dare look in the bleachers where about two thousand monsters of all kinds waited for the game to start. His dad must be up there, watching. Karl could only imagine how mad he must be.

The Werewolves were already lined up on the field. They were sleek in their perfectly sewn black uniforms. Alphonse mouthed the words, "Hi, Poo-dle."

He didn't realize he'd stopped in his tracks until Coach Wyatt gave him a nudge. "Hustle, Karl."

The first note of the anthem played just as Karl stepped into a line with his teammates. The Scream Team was about to play its first game.

CHAPTER 9
First Pitch

"Welcome to opening night, fiends and neighbors!" Hairy Hairwell, the announcer, cried from his booth. "The makers of Bursting Brains, the candy that smarts when you crunch it, present JC Monster League Baseball!"

Hairy waited for the crowd's cheers to die down and then continued, "Tonight's game at Putridge Stadium is between the Werewolves . . ."

The crowd cheered again.

". . . and the Scream Team!" Hairy shouted.

Silence from the bleachers, except for a few people asking each other, "Who? The *what* team? And why are they wearing coffin liners?"

Karl tried to block out the voices as he and the rest of the Scream Team scurried to the dugout. They'd never even played a scrimmage. And now they were about to play an actual league game. Karl felt like throwing up. Everything he'd done had been leading up to this moment.

"All right, gang," Coach Virgil said and held up a baseball. "As sure as this ball is filled with rat gut, I believe in you." He held up a glass of sludge. "As sure as this is the most delicious drink, you are the most delicious team. As sure as a three-headed elbow eater has—"

"Oh brother," Wyatt interrupted with a groan.

"Excuse me, bro," Virgil said. "I was giving an inspirational speech."

Wyatt rolled his eyes. "Is inspirational another word for boring?"

This was going nowhere. They had to get out on

the field and warm up. Karl finally said, "Let's win the game, Scream Team!" The players rushed out of the dugout and onto the field.

Dennis nibbled on his mitt at first. Eric quivered at second. Patsy was at shortstop. And Maxwell was unraveling at third. Out at left field was Mike. The center fielder was Bolt, and right fielder was Beck.

Just as Karl got in place at home plate, Hairy Hairwell announced, "We're waiting for our umpire, the all-seeing Frank the Cyclops. He's about to say the words all monsters love to hear—"

"Play ball!" the umpire cried.

With that, the game officially started!

The fans hooted and cheered as a Werewolf named Bennett strolled to the plate and got into his stance. He was a huge wolf with a cold stare.

On the mound, J.D. gave Karl a scared nod. He was ready . . . at least kind of. Karl glanced at the Coaches Conundrum to see what pitch they wanted.

Wyatt touched his nose and then tapped their chest.

Virgil scratched an ear and pulled his ponytail.

Oh no, Karl thought, *they aren't going to send opposite signals all game, are they?*

"Pick a pitch, please!" he yelled.

"Sorry, dude," Virgil called back. "I was just scratching an itch."

Karl put one finger down and touched his left leg. A signal for a fastball. J.D. nodded again. In his chest, visible to everyone, his heart started racing—very fast.

J.D. pulled back his left arm for the windup.

"It's going to be a fastball!" Alphonse yelled from the Werewolf dugout.

Bennett adjusted his stance just as J.D. fired off his pitch. The ball sailed right in the batter's wheelhouse. He swung, and—*whack!* The ball rocketed out into center field. Bolt's arm that had belonged to a gardener was busy picking dandelions as the ball bounced next to him.

But Mike got a flipper on it, covering it with slime. He tossed the ball to first.

By the time Dennis wiped it off and threw the ball to Maxwell at third, the Werewolf had been there and left. As his paws crossed over home plate, Karl's heart sank.

"Home run!" Hairy Hairwell yelled. "And that's just the first pitch. Boys and ghouls, we're about to see this new Scream Team get creamed!"

Karl could see Coach Powers agreed with Hairy. He had his paws up in the dugout, telling jokes to his players. He wasn't even watching the game.

Next up was Zoe, a left-pawed Werewolf. J.D. dug into the rosin bag he kept behind the mound. Then the ghost set his mitt at the home plate, wound up—

"It's a changeup!" Alphonse shouted just as J.D. let go of the ball.

Zoe switched her stance. And *crack!* She nailed a hard line drive down the right field line.

Beck stood up on his toes to catch it. This almost doubled his height. Now he had to reach *down* to get the ball. It bounced off his glove into the grass. He grabbed it and made the throw to Eric at second.

But Zoe was already at third—and then on her way to home.

"Home run!" Hairy bellowed over the speakers. "Two pitches and two home runs!"

"Spies!" Coach Wyatt yelled. "They have spies on our team!"

But Karl didn't think spies were the reason

Alphonse knew what J.D. was going to pitch. It was J.D. himself. You could tell what he was thinking just by watching his heart beat.

"J.D.!" Karl called out to him. "You're giving yourself away. Think about something other than pitching!"

"Like what?" J.D. asked. "I'm the *pitcher*!"

Karl called for a slow ball. J.D.'s heart slowed down as he wound up—

"Slow ball!" Alphonse shouted and the batter hit a single. Werewolves were now on first and second.

The next batter whacked a grounder. Patsy snagged the ball. She touched her heel to second. Her foot snapped off, but her momentum kept going. She whipped the ball to first.

"Don't throw so hard!" Dennis shrieked. He popped into a bat, his mitt falling on first base. Luckily, the ball landed in the glove.

"Around the horn!" Hairy called. "A double play!"

Karl felt a rush of excitement. Two outs just like that!

But the Scream Team didn't hold them for long. The Werewolves scored one more run before Mike caught a pop fly for the third out.

The rest of the Scream Team cheered. But Karl just stared at the scoreboard. The Werewolves were already up three to zip—and his dream of winning the game was slipping away.

CHAPTER 10
Think, Don't Think

As the game headed into the bottom of the first, Alphonse strutted out to the pitcher's mound. He made the number one sign with one paw and pointed to the #1 on his uniform with the other paw. The crowd loved it.

"Alphonse is the best pitcher in the JCML," Hairy Hairwell gushed. "This mighty Werewolf has thrown no-hitters in the last two scrimmages. And he looks ready to continue his streak tonight!"

Hairy was right. The first three batters for the

Scream Team were Beck, Mike, and Maxwell. And all three struck out. Just like that, the first inning was over.

"You guys need to focus!" Wyatt told the team back in the dugout.

"No, man, think less," Virgil said. "Just go with it. Empty your head."

"You're an expert on that, Virgil." Wyatt scowled.

The second and third innings didn't go much better for the Scream Team. Strikeout after strikeout. It wasn't until the fourth inning that their luck changed.

Patsy was at bat, her body tense, her face worried.

"Remember, think!" Wyatt called.

"Don't think!" Virgil shouted at the same time.

With the coaches shouting think and don't think at her, Patsy looked even more nervous for a second. And then she laughed. "You guys are hilarious."

Karl could see her relax.

"Okay, okay," she said. "I got this."

Alphonse pitched, trying to give her the brushback,

getting her off balance. She swung anyway—and connected! It was a soft roller toward third. She started to run. Her right leg snapped off. She grabbed her leg and had to hop the rest of the way to first. But she was on base!

The Scream Team cheered.

Next up was Dennis. "Hey, Bat Boy!" a Vampire in the bleachers yelled. "Are you and that bat in your hands related?"

Dennis blushed as he waddled to home plate.

"Just laugh, Dennis!" Patsy told him from first. "Laugh, and it won't seem so bad. Trust me!"

But Dennis was too freaked out. His face was scrunched up. Karl could tell he was trying not to turn into a bat. Alphonse threw three quick pitches.

The ump yelled, "Strike three! You're out!" Dennis rushed back to the dugout trying to hide the tears on his face. Maxwell unraveled some of his wrappings for him to use as a tissue. Dennis blew his nose in them.

"Don't worry," Karl patted him on the back. And his hand felt something. "Check it out, Dennis. You've got your bat wings."

Dennis looked over his shoulder. Two tiny wings sprouted from his back.

"I only turned partway into a bat, I guess!" he said, eyes wide.

Eric was up to bat next. Alphonse tried giving the blob the brushback. But the low and wide fastball sank right into Eric. He absorbed it like a sponge taking in water.

"Walk!" the ump called and waggled a finger at Alphonse. "Watch it, Werewolf."

"It's not my fault!" Alphonse cried. "These losers shouldn't even be out on the field!"

With Scream Team runners at first and second, it was Karl's turn at bat.

He spotted something out of the corner of his eye. Had Alphonse already pitched the ball? Karl swung the bat ... just as he realized he was swinging at his tail.

"Strike one!" the ump shouted.

"Still chasing your tail, Karl?" Alphonse asked from the mound. He fired off a pitch. Karl didn't swing, thinking it was a little high.

The ump called, "Strike two!"

"Good thing you got only one bad eye!" Wyatt

yelled at the ump before Virgil could clamp a hand over his mouth. "Sorry about that, Mr. Cyclops!" Virgil shouted.

A second later, Alphonse pulled back his arm and let loose with a screaming curveball. Karl focused all of his attention on the ball. He hit a grounder that bounced into left field.

Karl raced to first. He was on base! And Patsy and Eric had advanced to second and third.

"Wicked, Karl!" Virgil shouted.

Up next, Bolt hit a fly ball that bounced to the turf just between center and left field. The Werewolves scrambled, and Karl was tagged out at third—

But by then, Patsy had sprinted to home plate, with Eric right on her heels, bouncing like a Super Ball.

Yes! Karl pumped a paw in the air.

"What's this?" Hairy Hairwell said over the loudspeaker. "I don't believe it! The Scream Team is on the board!"

CHAPTER 11
Ghost of a Chance

As the score changed to 2 to 4, Karl saw all the joking around in the Werewolf dugout change, too. The Werewolves were still up by two. But Coach Powers was standing now, shouting and pointing furiously at his players on the field.

The Scream Team's momentum didn't last long. J.D. was up next.

All the organs in J.D.'s see-through body pointed between first and second as he slugged out a grounder. So the Werewolf shortstop had been waiting. He easily snagged the ball and J.D. was out at first.

The top of the fifth inning started with the Werewolf Francis at bat, a true power hitter. Coach Wyatt called for a curveball.

J.D.'s heart skipped a few beats as he got ready to throw.

"Curveball," Alphonse announced, sounding almost bored with being able to read J.D. like a book. Francis hit an easy single.

With the next batter—a Werewolf named Albert—J.D. took his time with the rosin bag. He was about to toss the bag behind him again, when he stopped and looked at his dust-covered fingers. Getting an idea, he dumped the white chalk over his head.

As the crowd laughed and the Werewolves howled, J.D. wound up for the pitch.

"Uh . . ." Alphonse said from the dugout. With J.D. covered in white dust, Alphonse couldn't tell from the beating of his heart what the pitch would be anymore.

J.D. delivered. The Werewolf swung and connected with nothing but air. One strike. Now that Alphonse couldn't shout out the pitches, the Werewolves would have to play to win.

With two strikes, Albert finally managed to hit one of J.D.'s pitches. It sailed to the outfield.

Beck ran for it, looking like a scuba diver on land. He tripped and landed on his back. Hard. The ball bounced about twenty feet away.

Beck kicked his legs in frustration. His flipper feet were like fans. Suddenly, he was gliding across the grass like a hovercraft on the water.

"Wahoo!" he shouted, surprised.

Beck zipped to the ball and threw it to the infield, stopping Francis at third.

In the eighth inning, Mike got the
Scream Team off to an amazing start.

Alphonse growled at him from the mound. But
Mike didn't cower. Instead, he followed Patsy's lead.
He laughed.

Mike switched from gripping the bat with his
hands to using his tail. His stance seemed much
more natural now.

Alphonse put everything he had behind the
pitch, but it wasn't enough. Mike whacked a double
out of it.

"Swamp thing, that's some swing!" Virgil shouted
to him.

Maxwell strutted out to the field swinging
the bat. Unfortunately, he was heading toward
the bathrooms. Karl turned him around, and the
mummy made his way to home plate.

"I guess it's time for me to give up a little fashion
for the team," Maxwell said before Karl trotted back
to the dugout. Maxwell pushed aside some of the
wrapping on his face so he could see better.

Now when the pitch came, he nailed it. He hit another double and Mike raced home.

Still covered in the white powder from the rosin bag, J.D. went to bat. Alphonse stared at him for a second, trying to read inside his body. But all he got was a grin and a laugh back from J.D.

"Balllaahhhhsh!" J.D. told Alphonse with a grin. "I'm going to gobble up this pitch!"

And he did. He powered out a line drive that bounced to left field. He raced around the bases. Maxwell tore home—and then J.D!

Blam! Blam!

When they crossed home plate, it put the Scream Team someplace Karl never thought they'd be—

They were in the lead!

The score was 5 to 4.

Hairy Hairwell seemed just as shocked. "If the Scream Team can hold the Werewolves and keep them from scoring another run," he announced, "they could actually win this game!"

CHAPTER 12
Karl's Call

By the ninth inning, it was clear the Scream Team might be a bunch of misfits. But many had shown they had something special to offer.

Not me, though, Karl thought miserably.

In his two other turns at bat, he'd hit a dribbler back to the mound and a hot shot in the hole fielded by the shortstop. Both easy outs. And as catcher—he was anything but special. He kept dropping balls and flubbing throws.

With only one inning left, he still hadn't found a

way to impress Coach Powers. He crouched down behind home plate and hoped he'd have the chance.

J.D. fired off a fastball, and Albert nailed this one. But it was a spitball straight to Mike's mitt.

Ronnie, a big left-pawed Werewolf, stormed out to the batting box. The infield was back, because they knew that Ronnie could run. J.D. delivered. Ronnie swung, hitting a ground ball half speed going down to second.

Maxwell charged it, missed it with his mitt. But slung out a strip of sweaty cloth from his other arm—hooking the ball and pulling it back to him. The Werewolf on third decided to stay put.

"That's what I'm talking about!" Virgil shouted.

"No," Wyatt said. "That's what *I'm* talking about!"

With two outs, the bases were loaded with Werewolves now. Just one more run, and the score would be tied. And the Scream Team's lead would be gone.

Alphonse pushed past Karl and stepped to the plate.

"Watch this," he said to Karl with a wink.

Alphonse tapped his bat to the dirt and then pointed it out past the outfield.

"I can't believe it!" Hairy Hairwell shouted. "Alphonse is saying he's ready to fill the mighty shoes of Wolfenstein!"

Karl couldn't believe what he was seeing either. *Fill the shoes of Wolfenstein?* he thought. *No way, not on my watch.*

J.D. waited for the call. Karl looked at the Coaches. Wyatt touched his nose. Virgil tugged an ear. One wanted a fastball and the other a changeup. They both kept tapping a nose and tugging an ear. Karl didn't know what to do.

"Let's move along, Scream Team," the ump finally said.

Karl panicked for a second. And then an idea for a throw popped into his head. They didn't have a signal for it, so he just shouted, "Ding-dong!" and hoped that J.D. would understand.

Alphonse laughed. "Ding-dong? I know J.D. is one, but the guy is on your team."

After a quick nod to Karl, J.D. let loose. The pitch's path had a corkscrew in the center—just like when J.D. threw the ball at the Conundrums' doorbell. The backdoor slider curved just in time to cross over the plate. Alphonse got nothing but air. *Whift!*

"Strike one!" the umpire shouted.

Alphonse grunted angrily and got back in his stance. J.D. tried the same pitch again. This time Alphonse connected. A hard line drive going down the right field line, it was a foul ball by a few feet.

Two strikes. Two outs. The bases were loaded and Karl knew everything was riding on this next throw. The "ding-dong" pitch had taken some of the steam out of Alphonse's swagger. But now he was ready for it. "You know what they say, third time's the charm," he growled to Karl.

Karl glanced at the Coaches. They were still fighting over which pitch to call. Karl decided now was the time to give J.D. a chance. Karl had to let go of his pitching dream if he wanted the bigger one to come true.

"Your choice, J.D.," Karl said. "You're the pitcher. You know best."

J.D. was covered with white dust but there was no hiding the deep-red blush that covered his body. "Thanks, Karl," he said.

The Werewolf runners took their leads. J.D. set his mitt at the target zone and let loose. With any other hitter, the screaming fastball would have been a strike. But Alphonse was the best hitter in the league.

He belted a long drive heading between center and right field—to the bleachers. Bolt was there with his head down, helping a giant worm dig a hole.

"It's going right where Alphonse pointed," Hairy Hairwell announced. "The Werewolves will win! They will win!"

No, Karl thought, *not this time*.

He shouted, "Who knows what 145 divided by 234 is?"

Bolt's head was still down, but his teacher's pet arm shot up. And started waving like it knew the answer. The ball ricocheted off Bolt's glove. It hit the ground and bounced toward first, heading high over Dennis's head and at the bleachers.

Dennis closed his eyes. Two tiny wings popped up on his back. He flapped them like a hummingbird. His flight lasted just a second—but long enough for him to snag the ball. He should have touched first. But instead he fired the ball blindly back into the infield toward second.

It was yet another error for the Scream Team. The Werewolf running from third to home slowed down to enjoy the ride. Smiling, he watched as the ball was about to sail over Patsy's head.

Patsy yanked off her hand that wore the mitt. She tossed them in the air, and the ball knocked into the mitt. The ball fell, and Eric rolled beneath it. The ball rebounded off him and zinged toward home plate.

By now, the Werewolf runner heading home had seen the danger and picked up speed. He was sprinting straight at Karl. And so was the ball.

It was up to Karl to make an impossible catch.

"Poo-dle! Poo-dle!" he heard Alphonse start

to chant. A few Werewolves in the dugout started making squeaking sounds to distract Karl.

That did it. Karl couldn't take any more.

He dropped his mitt and flipped up his catcher's mask.

"Mr. and Mrs. Monster and all the monsters of the sea, the catcher is dumbstruck!" Hairy Hairwell shouted. "The Scream Team catcher is giving up!"

CHAPTER 13
No Excuses

Karl heard Hairy Harwell's shouting voice.

But he wasn't listening. He wasn't listening to anyone else. Not Coach Powers. Not Alphonse. Just himself for once.

Two objects were zipping his way. One was a ball. The other was a Werewolf barreling toward Karl like a freight train. The Werewolf bellowed, "I'm coming home, Poodle! Out of my way!"

Karl opened his mouth. He kept his eyes locked on the ball. It flew the last few inches—

Karl did what he had always fought against.

He chased the ball.

He leapt into the air and caught the ball between his teeth. With a spin, he reached out and tagged the Werewolf runner.

"You're out!" the ump cried.

The air was electric. Like the moment just before lightning struck. Then Hairy Hairwell shouted over and over:

"The Scream Team wins the game! The Scream Team wins the game!"

Almost without thinking, Karl turned to look for his dad in the stands. But before he could spot him, he was mobbed by his eight teammates. They hoisted him into the air and bounced him up and down.

"You did it, Karl!" J.D. shouted. "Number zero is a hero!"

On his perch of victory, Karl enjoyed the view. He turned his face up and drank in the moonlight. So this is what it felt like to win.

Coaches Conundrum pushed their way through the Scream Team. Virgil gave him the thumbs-up and said, "I told you no one had seen what you can do."

"All right, all right already," Wyatt said. "Let's not give him a big head." But when Karl looked down from the shoulders of his friends, Wyatt was actually smiling. Or at least trying to.

"Coach is right," Karl said. "Give someone else a chance up here!"

Eric was next. They bounced him around like a shimmering beach ball. He was quivering with joy.

They broke off the celebration to shake limbs with the Werewolves.

When Karl got to Alphonse, he slapped his paw and said, "Good game." But the big werewolf had nothing to say. He just rolled his eyes and kept on moving.

At the end of the line, Coach Powers waited for Karl. He pulled him over to the side. "That was an okay game, Karl," he said.

Karl smiled. "Thanks, Coach."

Coach Powers held up a paw. "Don't get carried away. Your win was a fluke, and you know it." He gave Karl a long look and said, "Still, I have an offer to make to you."

Here we go!

"Just admit that this whole multi-monster Scream Team idea was silly," Coach Powers told him. "And we'll get you in a real uniform with a real team. You can be a Werewolf."

Karl's ears perked up. Not only because of what Coach Powers had said but because he could hear Patsy talking with the Zombie coach. And over there J.D was meeting with the coach of the Ghosts. He knew those coaches were inviting them on the teams.

This is what we all wanted.

But maybe not anymore. At least not for Karl.

"Coach," Karl said, "I know how you feel about excuses. So I won't make any for the Scream Team. In fact, I couldn't if I tried. I'm too proud of them."

Coach Powers stared at him as if he couldn't believe his ears. "Karl, don't make a big mistake. You had a lucky game tonight."

"I had a *fun* game tonight," Karl said. "Thanks for the offer, but I'm going to stick with my friends."

As Karl turned away from Coach Powers, he spotted his dad up in the stands. He was sitting by himself, and he had the proudest wolf's grin on his face.

Karl would meet up with him in the parking lot. In the meantime, he headed back to the Scream Team celebration. His teammates were laughing and slapping each other's backs. Karl asked Patsy what happened with the Zombie coach.

"He invited me on the team," she said seriously.

"And what'd you say?" Karl asked.

She smiled. "That I wasn't interested. Maybe I'm losing my head. Again. But I want to stay with you guys."

Drifting over to them J.D. chimed in, "I just told the Ghosts there's no way I'm leaving the Scream Team."

"That's monstrous!" Karl howled. "I think we've got a winning season ahead of us!"

After the team dumped the traditional bucket of boiling slime on the Coaches Conundrum, Virgil shouted, "You guys are wicked!"

"Just like always," Wyatt scoffed at his brother. "You're dead wrong."

Karl and the rest of the team groaned. The Conundrums couldn't fight about this, too, could they?

"The Scream Team isn't just wicked," Wyatt said. "It's the *most* wicked!"

Scream Team

KARL THE WEREWOLF

Number: 0 Meant to be 9 but forgot the tail... so okay, I'm 0

Position: Catcher Wanted to be pitcher

Throws: Right

Bats: Likes them! Dennis the vampire is cool

Hobby: Collects grass clippings and hot dog skin! from baseball games

Favorite Food: Grandma's Spicy Road Kill with extra crispy whiskers

Baseball Hero: Wolfenstein of the Monster League Werewolves & home run Globe Series champ

Favorite saying: Wolfsbane! Only when things go bad!

Place to Improve: Chasing own tail or anything that squeaks

Talent: Really sinks his teeth into the game Ha!

Nickname: ~~Poodle~~ Wolfenstein II?

STILL HUNGRY?

Sink your teeth into:

The Vampire at Half Court

Guess what, sports fangs? Basketball season is here! That's right. . . . Karl and the rest of the misfit monsters are back to dribble, drool, and decay up and down the court — but not everyone is happy to see them. A plan is hatched to split up the Scream Team and keep them from winning the big championship. To add to the hoopla, it looks like Dennis might be switching teams and joining the Vampires! Can Karl keep the squad together long enough to net a victory? Find out in the second, action-packed book in the Scream Team series!